JOHN BLAIR
AND THE
GREAT HINCKLEY FIRE

Josephine Nobisso

Illustrated by Ted Rose

Houghton Mifflin Company

To the family, friends, and fellow pilgrims
with whom I've passed through fire of a very different nature.
—J.N.

To the memory of Fred's father
—T.R.

www.hmco.com/trade

The text of this book is set in New Century Schoolbook.
The illustrations are watercolors, reproduced in full color.

Library of Congress Cataloging-in-Publication Data

Nobisso, Josephine.
John Blair and the great Hinckley fire / by Josephine Nobisso ; illustrated by Ted Rose.
p.   cm.
Summary: Tells how a brave African American porter helped save many lives when the train
on which he was working was caught up in the horrendous firestorm near Hinckley, Minnesota, in 1894.
ISBN 0-618-01560-4
1. Forest fires — Minnesota — Hinckley Region — History — 19th century — Juvenile literature.
2. Hinckley Region (Minn.) — History — 19th century — Juvenile literature.
3. Blair, John Wesley — Juvenile literature. 4. Afro-American train attendants — Minnesota —
Hinckley Region — Biography — Juvenile literature. [1. Forest fires. 2. Blair, John Wesley. 3. Heroes.
4. Afro-Americans — Biography. 5. Railroad accidents.] I. Rose, Ted, ill. II. Title.
F614.H6N63   2000
977.6'62 — dc21
99-33251
CIP

Manufactured in the United States of America
WOZ 10 9 8 7 6 5 4 3 2 1

Author Acknowledgments

Laura E. Rust, researcher, St. Paul, who, at 76, was my indefatigable right hand and better eye in Minnesota. Jeanne Coffey, curator, Hinckley Fire Museum, for her help out of season. Hampton Smith and Steve Nielson, research librarians, and the Minnesota Historical Society, for their patient research. Barbara Dewey, librarian, Chapel Hill, North Carolina, for widening the path she'd traversed before me. Jerry Horn and Robert Allard, reference librarians, Westhampton Free Library, and all the library staff, for their ever-cheerful assistance. Margaret Raymo, senior editor, Houghton Mifflin, who asked me to find out more. Chicago Historical Society, for research materials.

STEAM HISSED ONTO THE RAILROAD PLATFORM IN DULUTH. John Blair helped more passengers, a lady with seven excited and perspiring children, onto the train. From the steps of his car, John took another look at the ominous sky. It was smudged with dirty clouds, the debris of forest fires. Every summer, huge sections of timber burned throughout Minnesota, blocking the sun. Some years the rangers recorded more than two thousand fires. This sultry September first in 1894 seemed no different from others.

Conductor Thomas Sullivan called out, "All aboard!" Although it was as dusky as dinner time in winter, The Limited, Train No. 4, was right on time: 1:55 in the afternoon. The train would make the 170-mile run southward to St. Paul in five hours, with a halfway stop at Hinckley. At the end of the line, John Blair would go home to dinner with his wife and two boys.

With a cough and bursts of steam, the locomotive started the massive train rolling until it was clickety-clacking down the tracks.

A porter for the St. Paul and Duluth Railway Company, John was to attend to the needs of about 150 passengers that hot Saturday afternoon. In his calm, easy way, he passed through two coaches, two chair cars, and the smoking car, exchanging pleasantries with the passengers, many of whom were regulars. By the time the whistle shrieked through Carlton, John noticed trees burning on both sides of the tracks.

It was three o'clock when the train raced through Barnum, but it looked as dark as midnight. John's passengers were getting nervous. He began lighting every lamp, speaking reassuringly as he went. When people complained of suffering from the smoke, John brought towels from the porter's cabinet into the washroom, soaking them as the train raced southward.

Suddenly a red glow flashed in the washroom mirror. John ducked back into the compartment to see his passengers' faces frozen in scarlet terror. Looking out from the vestibule, he saw that the trees on both sides of the train were blazing. Flames swirled up trunks that snapped off and lifted, becoming burning arrows. Gasps went up as trees crashed against the train, exploding in showers of sparks.

The train lurched. There was a terrible silence, and then everyone began talking at once. The engine gathered steam and sped onward. "No cause for concern, folks," John consoled. "We're out of that scrape!"

At last, as The Limited approached Miller, the air grew less dense. Mothers stroked their children's sweaty brows, and Senator Daugherty, traveling with his ten-year-old son, said, "As long as we're moving, Otto, all will be well." But as the train roared past the Miller depot, John noticed that the alarmed faces of the people gathered there were lit by an unnatural yellow light.

Seven minutes from Hinckley, the train crossed over the culvert spanning Skunk Lake. A foul-smelling spot where snakes and insects bred, Skunk Lake was the only water hole within fifteen miles of the tracks. West of the embankment, the swamp lay shallow and muddy, but on the east side, it opened up into a deep murky pond.

When the train was a mile from Hinckley, the air cleared and cooled, as if all the debris had been sucked away. "Trouble's behind us now," John said. As he opened a window, the train came to a dead stop. John peered out, wondering what had made the engineer, Jim Root, pause this far from the station.

An astonishing sight made John's breath catch. He ran to the door. Men, women, and children, clothes half burned, bodies covered in ashes and soot, came groaning and crying out of the woods. "For God's sake!" they pleaded with Engineer Root. "Can you save us?"

John reached into the outstretched hands, lifting people into his car, soothing them, handing them into the care of his passengers, who'd come forward. Out of the forests and over the hill more people appeared, thrashing at the barbed-wire fences. They boarded, exhausted and burned, crying and babbling about fire. A dog, yelping, his tail between his legs, came bounding aboard, but still no one on the train could see any fire.

"What's the trouble in Hinckley?" Engineer Root shouted as he helped hoist sobbing people onto the train. The Bartletts, who ran the eating house at the depot, were among the last to be pulled aboard. Mr. Bartlett gasped as he spoke: "Everything's burned up! Everything's on fire! The depot! The track house! Your bridge is down! There's no getting through here!"

With fire ahead and fire behind, there was nothing to do but find refuge between the two and pray for the best. "We'll go back to Skunk Lake," Root told his crew.

John turned to prepare his passengers to reenter the fearsome territory they'd just left. It would certainly be worse now; the fire might even have reached Skunk Lake.

"We'll never get there alive!" Sullivan cried.

"Then we'll be dying together, Thomas," the engineer answered soberly.
Jim Root climbed the engine and hauled on the levers. With a burst of steam,
The Limited backed up, stopping and starting to take on more refugees until
Jim felt they could do so no longer. He reversed at breakneck speed, his train
packed to the aisles with more than three hundred passengers, all of them
terrified, half of them injured.

John Blair faced a terrible scene. Women clutching babies screamed for their other children. Neighbor begged neighbor for news of family members. Men shouted out loved ones' names, only to sob when no response came. Settlers who'd come out of the woods to fight small fires in town sank to their knees, begging John to stop the train so they could fetch their families. John thought of his own wife and sons, and of how all these people were depending on him.

A great, strange roar rose up. The people from Hinckley let out screams as the other passengers tried to fathom what it was. Suddenly trees and debris were shooting past the windows. Winds slammed the train at hurricane speed, rocking the cars as if they were toys.

John's eyes widened. A wall of fire, sky-high and as dense as a sea, barreled toward them, its red flames churning. The very air around the speeding train seemed to ignite then, sounding one huge explosion. Fire engulfed the train. The baggage car burst into flames and the windows imploded. Broken glass melted and curtains disintegrated into red spider lace. In panic over the families they'd left behind, two settlers dove out into the tidal wave of fire.

People screamed, pressing into the aisle as the end of the train caught fire, and the tender—the fuel car—loaded with coal, ignited. Fire licked up from beneath John's car, feeding on axle grease. Through the transoms, flames reached in, setting hair aflame.

John climbed over seats and hefted the fire extinguisher off the floor. Singed and blistered himself, he sprayed his passengers' clothing, swirling in the firestorm's wind. Over the roar of the cyclone, John shouted, "Lie down! For pity's sake, get down!" The floor would be scorching, but down there, in less wind, he'd have a chance to douse the people's clothing. The car felt like the inside of a cooking stove, but John continued to work the extinguisher. Flames darted in through all sides. John's hands swelled to twice their size and blistered so badly that the flesh was rubbing off.

He leaped to the washroom to help the railway superintendent, who was filling containers with water. The people passed these around, taking great gulps for their burning throats and then dousing children's heads. They distributed the sopping towels John had wet earlier, using them to wrap people's burns.

When the train lurched, a great gasp went up. "It's off the tracks! It's the end!" someone yelled. Otto cried, "Papa, do we have to die? Do we?"

John wondered if fallen trees had caused Jim to reduce steam. It would be another day before he learned that a shard of glass had cut the engineer's throat, making him bleed until he'd fainted across the throttle, almost shutting down the train. The Limited was crawling backward now, rocking in the inferno.

A man crazed with terror clutched John, demanding, "Why don't you put the fire out?"

His eyes stinging and smarting, his lungs parched, John instructed his passengers to stay calm.

Except for their gasping, everyone in the car grew strangely quiet. In the wind the undercarriage creaked and the seats squeaked. John sprayed people huddled in the aisle. Children sobbed quietly. Mothers rocked them, dazed and in shock. Most of the passengers showed an astonishing calm, steeled for the worst and praying deeply as blinding fireballs shot overhead, sending deafening showers onto the train's roof. A thick blizzard of flakes was swirling through, burning red before turning black. John put out fire after fire in people's clothing while his mind raced, wondering why they were only inching along.

Suddenly, because Engineer Root had regained consciousness and opened the throttle full-steam backward, No. 4 came to life again, careening and screaming along the hot tracks.

Soon the engine hissed to a stop. Black smoke poured into the train. Someone cried out, "This is the place!" People rushed to exit, not realizing they were facing west, where the swamp water was lower. Sullivan came running, a pail in hand, sloshing water over the scorching metal steps. The dog darted between John's legs, leaping off.

John helped passengers as they jumped onto the parched grass. He carried women and children, planting them on their feet before rushing back for others. Someone flung a baby out the window, and a man caught her outside. The railroad's barbed-wire fence was kicked down. People, eyes blinded and smarting, clutched each other, rushing into the mud, sinking into the shallow, putrid water.

John could barely force his swollen eyes open, but he dragged two fire extinguishers out of the train. He led the last of the staggering passengers into the marsh. Just then the passenger car burst into flames, the wind knocking people into the mire. What was left, twisted and blackened metal, crashed to the ground.

The three hundred people crowded in the swamp covered themselves with stagnant water and thick mire that reflected the awful red of the burning forest. John noticed that wind-borne fire sweeps were coming in a pattern: as one approached, people heard its roar, screamed, and crouched in time. When it passed, their heads surfaced so that they could breathe. The train must have arrived between two of these sweeps, giving the refugees just enough time to find shelter before the cars ignited in a blaze.

John figured that if he could stand up after each sweep barreled past, he'd have some moments to help people. He rose, dousing clothing and salvaging fabric scraps to cover exposed heads. Gradually the lapses between sweeps grew longer. When the forest fuel was used up, the fire lost its power and moved on.

Porter Blair helped his passengers onto the banks. He saw desolation everywhere. The fire had burned down to the subsoil, melting the sand into solid crusts in spots. Not even the stoutest tree was left standing. People sat, dazed, heads in their laps, swaying and moaning, calling for the loved ones who had not been with them on The Limited.

As night fell, the air became so cold that the refugees huddled beside the embers of what had once been the train that carried them to safety. Some joined Engineer Root on the hot metal engine. Eventually they all gathered on the swamp banks injured and exhausted, in shock and in need, while John Blair tended to them. Thomas Sullivan walked the tracks to find help.

Only three people who made it to Skunk Lake had died: two who'd refused to leave their seats and one who'd taken refuge in the eastern part of the lake, which, although deeper, had been licked down to sooty ash.

In the early morning gloom, a relief crew from Duluth trudged through on handcars, carrying them when they encountered mangled sections of track. They came to the ashes of what had been The Limited, and they removed their hats out of respect for the dead. They prepared to move on, but a crewman called out, in case even one dying person should answer. John, wrapping a man's burns, bobbed his head up. With one voice, he and the three hundred others called out, breaking the awful silence with a cry of relief and hope. Porter John Wesley Blair stood up, brushed off his muddy uniform, and climbed the embankment to give his report.

∽ EPILOGUE ∽

THE HINCKLEY FIRE OF 1894 WAS NOT A TYPICAL FOREST FIRE. INSTEAD, it was the most devastating fire phenomenon: a firestorm.

Regular forest fires burn relatively slowly, in "open-finger" patterns that allow people and animals to escape. They leave as much as a foot of charred debris on the forest floor. A firestorm, on the other hand, appears to ignite the gases in the very air that feeds it. Super-heating the atmosphere, it leaps along on exploding currents, consuming everything down to the subsoil.

Although much of the Hinckley fire occurred in remote backwoods where it is estimated that only 3,500 people lived, it claimed at least 413 lives, more than the famous fire of Chicago twenty-three years earlier. It devastated six towns, ravaging more than 400 square miles and 350,000 acres of timber. It burned so hot that isolated survivors were able to stave off starvation by eating potatoes that had baked in the ground. Of the 250 buildings in Hinckley, the ruins of only three were left, one of them the brick schoolhouse.

On September 13, 1894, the African-American community held a meeting in St. Paul to recognize the heroism of Porter John Wesley Blair, a man who is thought to have been born a slave in Arkansas. Judge O'Brien, the former mayor and a passenger on The Limited, Train No. 4, gave one of the many moving testimonials: "We stood in flame that is inde-scribable," he told the assembly. "John Blair might have sought his own safety, but he was too much a man for that. He stood there, a willing sacrifice, ready to lay down his life for those in his charge . . . following the dictates of a heart as pure and noble as any that ever beat in a human breast . . . never forgetting those who were helpless and who needed his assistance."

The community presented John with a handsome gold badge, purchased through a goodwill collection. On its front was a red-enameled engraving of a burning train. The rail-way authorities were last to pay tribute "for gallant and faithful discharge of duty on The Limited, Train No. 4," giving John a gold watch.

The monumental Hinckley fire, which raged more than a century ago and involved the very emblems of the American spirit—midwestern settlers, forests, and rail-roads — has left a lasting legacy, for from its devastation arose the forest fire monitoring program regulated by the U.S. Forest Service even today.